"Lively, often funny, and aphoristic . . . [*Bonsai*] holds stories within stories." —James Wood, *The New Yorker*

"Readers who consider Roberto Bolaño the pole star of contemporary Chilean fiction will be jolted by Zambra's little book. . . . Zambra is indeed the herald of a new wave of Chilean fiction." —*The Nation*

"A highly original work, full of unforgettable flashes of humor . . . brief as a sigh and forceful as a blow."
—*Capital*

"[*Bonsai*] is literature of the best kind, a work of strange maturity whose brevity is one of its greatest virtues—so much is said, and suggested, in so few pages." —*El Mercurio*

"A literary creation of the highest order . . . an unclassifiable object of unusual beauty . . . *Bonsai* is an exquisitely articulated work." —*Las Últimas Noticias*

"Undeniably fascinating . . . the kind of story that lingers in the mind for weeks after being read."
—*The Quarterly Conversation*

"What is remarkable about Zambra's novella is the space between ending and beginning—the progressive prose that relates a true story with emotional and artistic implications extending far beyond its eighty-three pages." —*Bookslut*

"*Bonsai* is an appealing miniature, a novella that, despite its brevity, feels airy and full . . . an enjoyable, pleasantly surprising, and clever read." —The Complete Review

"It is often said of a book that it is worth reading; rarely, as in [*Bonsai*'s] case, will a book be enjoyed even more in its rereading." —ABC España

# Praise for Alejandro Zambra

"Zambra's books have long shown him to be a writer who, at the sentence level, is in a world all his own. His exacting eye, his crack comic timing, his ability to describe just enough to keep the reader interested; these traits do much to demonstrate his staying power as an architect of larger stories." —NPR

"[Zambra's novels] are written with startling talent."
—*The New York Times Book Review*

"One of the most interesting writers working right now."
—*Elle*

"Zambra's sentences comically dance around narrative convention without disrupting the immersive pull of the story . . . and the effect is spellbinding. . . . His fiction is, quite simply, some of the best being produced today."

—*The Rumpus*

"If you are going to read Zambra, which you should, don't just read *My Documents*: read everything he's done."

—*The Guardian*

"Zambra is the author of small classics—short in length, but enormous in every other way."

—Valeria Luiselli, author of *Lost Children Archive*

"Zambra is so alert to the intimate beauty and mystery of being alive that in his hands a raindrop would feel as wide as a world."

—Anthony Marra, author of *The Tsar of Love and Techno*

"There is no writer like Alejandro Zambra, no one as bold, as subtle, as funny." —Daniel Alarcón, author of *The King Is Always Above the People*

"Zambra is the defining light of today's Latin American literature—an author whose cult is about to take over, the one we'll all be congratulating ourselves on having known about in the early days, before his deceptively slender masterpieces lay on every American reader's night table."

—John Wray, author of *Godsend*

"I read all of Alejandro Zambra's novels back-to-back because they were such good company. His books are like a phone call in the middle of the night from an old friend, and afterward, I missed the charming and funny voice on the other end, with its strange and beautiful stories."

—Nicole Krauss, author of *To Be a Man*

PENGUIN BOOKS

# BONSAI

Alejandro Zambra was born in Santiago, Chile, in 1975. He is the author of *Chilean Poet*, *Multiple Choice*, *Not to Read*, *My Documents*, *Ways of Going Home*, and *The Private Lives of Trees*. In Chile, among other honors, he has won the National Book Council Award for best novel three times. In English, he has won the English PEN Award and the PEN/O. Henry Prize and was a finalist for the Frank O'Connor International Short Story Award. He has also won the Prince Claus Award (Holland) and received a Cullman Center Fellowship from the New York Public Library. His books have been translated into twenty languages, and his stories have been published in *The New Yorker*, *The New York Times Magazine*, *The Paris Review*, *Granta*, *McSweeney's*, and *Harper's Magazine*, among other publications. He has taught creative writing and Hispanic literature for fifteen years and currently lives in Mexico City.

Megan McDowell (translator) is the recipient of a 2020 Award in Literature from the American Academy of Arts and Letters, among other awards, and has been short- or long-listed four times for the International Booker Prize.

# Bonsai

*Alejandro Zambra*

TRANSLATED BY

*Megan McDowell*

PENGUIN BOOKS

PENGUIN BOOKS
An imprint of Penguin Random House LLC
penguinrandomhouse.com

First English-language edition translated by Carolina De Robertis
published in the United States of America by
Melville House Publishing 2008
This new translation by Megan McDowell published in
Penguin Books 2022

Originally published in Spanish as *Bonsái* by Editorial
Anagrama, Barcelona.

Illustration by Leslie Leppe Gnecco

LIBRARY OF CONGRESS CATALOGING-IN-PUBLICATION DATA
Names: Zambra, Alejandro, 1975– author. |
McDowell, Megan, translator.
Title: Bonsai / Alejandro Zambra ; translated by Megan McDowell.
Other titles: Bonsái. English
Description: [New York] : Penguin Books, 2022. |
Originally published in Spanish as Bonsái by
Editorial Anagrama, Barcelona. |
Identifiers: LCCN 2022003255 (print) | LCCN 2022003256 (ebook) |
ISBN 9780143136507 (trade paperback) |
ISBN 9780525508021 (ebook)
Subjects: LCGFT: Romance fiction. | Novels.
Classification: LCC PQ8098.36.A43 B6513 2022 (print) |
LCC PQ8098.36.A43 (ebook) | DDC 863/.64—dc23/eng/20220209
LC record available at https://lccn.loc.gov/2022003255
LC ebook record available at https://lccn.loc.gov/2022003256

Printed in the United States of America
1  3  5  7  9  10  8  6  4  2

Set in Adobe Caslon Pro
*Designed by Alexis Farabaugh*

*For Alhelí*

The years passed, and the only person who never
changed was the girl in the pages of his book.

—YASUNARI KAWABATA


Pain is inscribed and described.

—GONZALO MILLÁN

# Bonsai

*I.*

# Entity

I n the end she dies and he is alone, although really he had been alone for some years before her death, before Emilia's death. Let's say her name is or was Emilia and that his name is, was, and will be Julio. Julio and Emilia. In the end Emilia dies and Julio does not. The rest is literature:

The first night they slept together it was by accident. There was a test in Spanish Grammar II, a subject neither of them was great at, but since they were young and in theory up for anything, they were even up for studying Spanish Grammar II at the Vergara twins' house. The study group ended up being bigger than originally planned: someone put on music, saying she always listened to music while she studied; someone else brought vodka, arguing it was hard for him to focus without vodka; and a third person went to buy oranges, because she found vodka without orange juice intolerable. By three in the morning they were all perfectly sloshed, so they decided to go to sleep. And although Julio would have preferred to spend the night with one of the Vergara twins, he resigned himself pretty quickly to sharing the tiny spare bedroom (i.e., the maid's room) with Emilia.

Julio didn't like how Emilia asked so many questions in class, and Emilia found it annoying that Julio passed his classes even though he hardly ever set foot on campus, but that night they both discovered the emotional affinities that any couple can discover if they only put their minds to it. Needless to say, they did very badly on the exam. A week later, for the makeup test, they studied with the Vergaras again, and again they slept together, even though this time there was no need to share a room, since the twins' parents were away in Buenos Aires.


Not long before she got mixed up with Julio, Emilia had decided that from then on she was going to fuck—what the Spanish call "follar"—and she would no longer make love with anyone or hook up with anyone, much less would she screw, or "culiar," as a Chilean would say. This is a Chilean problem, Emilia said to Julio, with a boldness she only displayed in the dark—though in a very low voice, of course: This is the problem with young Chileans. We're too young to make love, and in Chile, if you don't make love you can only culiar, but I don't want to screw you, I'd rather follar, I'd rather fuck you like they do it in Spain.

At that time Emilia had never been to Spain. Years later she would live in Madrid, a city where she'd do her fair share of fucking, though no longer with Julio, but rather, mostly, with Javier Martínez and with Ángel García Atienza and with Julián Alburquerque and even—though only once and a little under duress—with her Polish friend Karolina Kopeć. However, that night, this second night, Julio became Emilia's second sexual partner. Or, as mothers and certain psychologists say with some degree of hypocrisy, he became Emilia's "second man," while Emilia became Julio's first serious relationship. Julio had avoided serious relationships, hiding not from women but from seriousness, since by that point he knew that seriousness was every bit as dangerous as women, if not more so. Julio knew he was doomed to seriousness, and he tried, stubbornly, to thwart his serious fate, even as he stoically awaited that frightening and inevitable day when seriousness would come to settle in his life for good.

Emilia's first boyfriend—or "pololo," as Chileans say—was clumsy, but there was something authentic in his clumsiness. He made a lot of mistakes and almost always knew how to recognize and fix them, but some mistakes are impossible to fix, and the clumsy guy, Emilia's first, made one or two of these unforgivable mistakes. It's not worth getting into what they were.

The two of them were both fifteen when they started dating, but when Emilia turned sixteen and seventeen the clumsy boyfriend remained fifteen. And so on: Emilia turned eighteen and nineteen and twenty-four, and he stayed fifteen; she turned twenty-seven, twenty-eight, and he was still fifteen, right up until Emilia turned thirty. Emilia didn't celebrate any more birthdays after thirty, not because she started lying about her age, but because a few days after her thirtieth birthday, she aged no more, because, starting then, she was dead.

Emilia's second boyfriend was too white. With him, she discovered hiking, bike rides, jogging, and yogurt. It was in particular a time of abundant yogurt, and this, for Emilia, was important, because she was just emerging from a period of abundant pisco, of long, convoluted nights of pisco with Coke and pisco with lemon and even pisco on its own, neat, no ice. They fooled around a lot but they never went all the way, because he was really white and that made Emilia distrust him, even though she herself was very white, almost completely white, albeit with short, very black hair, it's true.

The third guy was really a jackass. From the start she knew the relationship was doomed to fail, but even so they lasted a year and a half, and he was her first sexual partner—her "first man"—when she was eighteen and he was twenty-two.

Between the third and the fourth there were several onetime dalliances that were largely motivated by boredom.

The fourth was Julio.

In accordance with a long-standing family tradition, Julio's sexual initiation was outsourced, for the price of ten thousand pesos, to Isidora, "cousin Isidora," who of course was not named Isidora and was not Julio's cousin. All the men of the family had gone to Isidora, a still-young woman with miraculous hips and a certain propensity for romanticism, who agreed to service them even though she was no longer a hooker, not a real one: these days—and she always found a way to clarify this—she worked as a lawyer's secretary.

Julio first met cousin Isidora when he was fifteen, and he went on meeting her over the following years, as a gift on special occasions, when he was insistent enough, or when his father's cruelty waned and gave way to the inevitable period of fatherly repentance, and then to the period of fatherly guilt, whose happiest symptom was financial largesse. Needless to say, Julio was inclined to fall in love with Isidora, he cared about her, and she, fleetingly tender toward the bookish boy who dressed all in black, treated him better than her other patrons, pampered him; in a way, she educated him.

It wasn't until he turned twenty that Julio started to approach women his own age with socio-sexual intentions; his success was limited, but still enough for him to decide to quit Isidora. To quit her, of course, the same way one quits smoking or betting on horse races. It wasn't easy, but for some months before that second night with Emilia, Julio had considered himself free of vice.

That second night, then, Emilia competed with a single rival, though Julio never actually compared them, partly because there was no possible comparison and also because Emilia came to be, officially, the only love of his life, and Isidora merely a previous, agreeable source of fun and suffering. When Julio fell in love with Emilia, all the fun and all the suffering that came before the fun and suffering that Emilia brought him became mere imitations of true fun and true suffering.

The first lie Julio told Emilia was that he had read Marcel Proust. He didn't usually lie about his reading, but that second night, when they both knew they were starting something, and that however long it lasted, this something was going to be important—that night, Julio deepened his voice, feigning intimacy, and said that, yes, he had read Proust when he was seventeen, during a summer in Quintero. By that time no one in his family summered in Quintero—not even Julio's parents, who had met at El Durazno Beach, ever went to Quintero, a lovely beach town that according to them just wasn't what it used to be, now that it had been overrun by the masses. Anyway, Julio said, at seventeen he had commandeered his grandparents' summerhouse so he could shut himself in and read *In Search of Lost Time*. It was a lie, of course: he *had* gone to Quintero that summer, and he *had* read a lot, but he'd read Jack Kerouac, Heinrich Böll, Vladimir Nabokov, Truman Capote, and Enrique Lihn, not Marcel Proust.

That same night, Emilia lied to Julio for the first time, and the lie was, also, that she'd read Marcel Proust. At first she merely agreed: I read Proust too. But then there was a long, pregnant pause, which wasn't an uncomfortable silence but rather an expectant one, so Emilia had to complete the story: I read it recently, just last year, it took me like five months, I was really busy, as you know, with classes. But I decided to read all seven volumes and those were truly the most important months of my life as a reader.

She used that expression: my life as a reader—she said that those had been, without a doubt, the most important months of her life as a reader.

In Emilia and Julio's story, in any event, there are more omissions than lies, and fewer omissions than truths, truths of the kind that are said to be absolute and tend to be uncomfortable. Over their time together, which wasn't long but was long enough, they confided in each other their least public desires and aspirations, their disproportionate feelings, their brief and exaggerated life stories. Julio confessed to Emilia things that only his psychologist should have known, and Emilia, in turn, made Julio into a kind of retroactive accomplice to every one of the decisions she had made over the course of her life. The time, for example, at fourte, when she'd decided to hate her mother: Julio listened attentively and offered the opinion that, yes, fourteen-year-old Emilia had made a good decision, no other decision had been possible, he would have done the same, and, certainly, if they'd been together back then, when they were fourteen, he definitely would have supported her.

Emilia and Julio's was a relationship riddled with truths, with personal disclosures that quickly built up a complicity they strove to see as unassailable. This is, then, a light tale that becomes heavy. This is the story of two student enthusiasts of the truth, aficionados of deploying words that seem like truth, of smoking endless cigarettes, and of enclosing themselves within the violent complacency of those who believe themselves better and purer than others, than that immense and detestable group called *everyone else*.

They quickly learned to read the same way, to think similarly, and to hide their differences. Very soon they comprised a vain private world. For a time, at least, Julio and Emilia managed to meld into a single entity. They were, in short, happy. There can be no doubt about that.

*II.*

# Tantalia

fter that they went on fucking, follando, as it were, in other people's houses and in motels where the sheets smelled like pisco sour. They fucked for a year and that year seemed short to them, though it was actually very long, an unusually long year, at the end of which Emilia went to live with Anita, her childhood friend.

Anita was no fan of Julio's—she thought he was arrogant and depressive—but she still had to put up with him at breakfast, since he was a permanent guest in the cramped and rather inhospitable apartment that Emilia and Anita shared. Once, maybe to prove to herself and her friend that deep down she didn't really dislike Julio, she even made him soft-boiled eggs, his favorite. What really bothered Anita about Julio was that he had changed her friend:

You changed my friend. She didn't used to be like that.
And have you always been like this?
Like what?
Like this, how you are.

Emilia, conciliatory and sympathetic, intervened. Why would you want to be with someone if they didn't change your life? She said that, and Julio was there when she said it: that life only made sense if you found someone who would change it, who would destroy your life as you knew it. Anita found the theory a little dubious, but she didn't argue. She knew that when Emilia used that tone there was no point in contradicting her.

J ulio and Emilia's quirks weren't just sexual (though they did have those), or emotional (though those abounded), but also literary, so to speak. One especially happy night, as a joke, Julio read aloud a Rubén Darío poem that Emilia acted out and trivialized until it became a blatantly sexual poem, a poem of explicit sex, complete with screams and orgasms. After that it became a habit, this reading out loud—quietly—every night before fucking. They read *The Book of Monelle* by Marcel Schwob, and *The Temple of the Golden Pavilion* by Yukio Mishima, both of which turned out to be reasonable sources of erotic inspiration. Very soon, though, the readings became remarkably more diverse: they read *A Man Asleep* and *Things* by Georges Perec, several stories by Juan Carlos Onetti and Raymond Carver, poems by Ted Hughes, Tomas Tranströmer, Armando Uribe, and Kurt Folch. They even read excerpts from Nietzsche and Emil Cioran.

One fine or perhaps very bad day, chance led them to the pages of *The Book of Fantasy* by Jorge Luis Borges, Adolfo Bioy Casares, and Silvina Ocampo. After envisioning crypts and doorless houses, after taking inventory of the traits of unnameable ghosts, they landed on "Tantalia," a short story by Macedonio Fernández that affected them deeply.

"Tantalia" is the tale of a couple who decide to buy a little plant to keep as a symbol of the love that binds them. Too late, they realize that if the plant dies, the love that binds them will die too. And since the love that binds them is immense and they aren't willing to sacrifice it for anything, they decide to lose the plant amid a crowd of identical plants. Then comes the desolation, the tragedy of knowing that now they can never find it again.

She and he, Macedonio's characters, had a plant of love and lost it. Emilia and Julio—who aren't exactly characters, though maybe it's best to think of them that way—have been reading before fucking for several months, and it's very pleasant, he thinks and she thinks, and at times they think it simultaneously: It's very pleasant, it's beautiful to read and talk a little about what we read before tangling our legs together. It's like working out.

It wasn't always easy to find some reason in the text, small as it may be, to fuck, but in the end they always managed to find a paragraph or verse that, randomly drawn out or perverted, would work, would titillate them. (They liked that word, *titillate*, that's why I'm including it here. They liked it as much as they liked being titillated.)

But this time was different:

I don't like Macedonio Fernández anymore, said Emilia, piecing the words together with inexplicable shyness as she caressed Julio's chin and part of his mouth.

And Julio: Me neither. I used to think he was funny, I liked him a lot, but not anymore. I'm over Macedonio.

They had read Macedonio's story in very soft voices, and they went on speaking softly:

It's absurd, like a dream.
I mean, it *is* a dream.
It's dumb.
What do you mean?
Nothing, just that it's absurd.

That should have been the last time Emilia and Julio fucked. But they kept going, in spite of Anita's continued complaints and the extreme disquiet that Macedonio's story had inspired in them. Maybe to gauge their disenchantment, maybe just to change the subject, from then on they turned exclusively to the classics. They discussed, as all dilettantes the world over have at some point discussed, the opening chapters of *Madame Bovary*. They classified their friends and acquaintances as Charleses or Emmas, and they also discussed how they themselves compared to the tragic Bovary family. There was no question in bed, since they both tried their hardest to seem like Emma, to be like Emma, to fuck like Emma, because there was no doubt about it, they agreed, Emma fucked unusually well, and she would have fucked even better in current conditions; in Santiago de Chile at the end of the twentieth century, Emma would have fucked even better than she did in the book. On those nights, the bedroom turned into a self-driving bulletproof carriage feeling its way through a beautiful and unreal city. Everyone else, the townspeople, jealously whispered details of the scandalous and fascinating romance that was going on inside.

But in other aspects of their lives they couldn't agree. They couldn't decide whether Emilia resembled Emma and Julio, Charles, or if both of them inadvertently smacked of Charles. Neither of them wanted to be Charles, no one ever wants to be like Charles, not even a little.

They abandoned the book with only fifty pages to go, trusting, perhaps, that they could now retreat into the stories of Anton Chekhov.

Things went badly for them with Chekhov, and a little better, oddly, with Kafka. But, as they say, the damage was done. After they read "Tantalia" the end was imminent, and of course they imagined and even acted out scenes that made their denouement more beautiful and sad, more unexpected.


It happened with Proust. They had put off reading Proust due to the unspeakable secret that, separately, bound each of them to the reading—or the non-reading—of *In Search of Lost Time*. Both of them had to pretend that the shared reading was in fact a much-anticipated rereading, so that when they came to one of the many passages that seemed especially memorable they changed the inflection of their voices or gazed at one another in an appeal to emotion, simulating an intense intimacy. On one occasion, Julio even allowed himself to assert that only now did he feel he was really reading Proust, and Emilia replied with a subtle and disconsolate squeeze of his hand.

Smart as they were, they went right past the episodes they knew were celebrated: The rest of the world was moved by that, I will be moved by this other thing. Before starting to read, they had taken the precaution of agreeing on how difficult it was for a reader of *In Search of Lost Time* to talk about their reading experience: It's one of those books that even after you read it, it's still on your to-be-read list, said Emilia. It's one of those books we'll reread forever, said Julio.

They made it to page 369 of *Swann's Way*. Specifically, to the following sentence:

> *To know a thing does not enable us, always, to prevent its happening, but after all the things that we know we do hold, if not in our hands, at any rate in our minds, where we can dispose of them as we choose, which gives us the illusion of a sort of power to control them.*

It is possible but would perhaps be excessive to relate this excerpt to the story of Julio and Emilia. It would be excessive because Proust's novel is riddled with sentences like this one. And also because there are still pages to go, because this story continues.

Or doesn't continue.

The story of Julio and Emilia continues, but it doesn't keep going.

It will end some years later, with Emilia's death; Julio, who doesn't die, who will not die, who hasn't died yet, continues, but decides not to keep going. Emilia too: For now she decides not to keep going, but she does continue. Then, after some years, she will neither continue nor keep going.

Knowledge of a thing cannot prevent it, but there are illusions, and this story, which is something of a story of illusions, goes like this:

They both knew that, as the saying goes, the ending was already written—their ending, that of the sad young people who read novels together, who wake up with books tangled in the blankets, who smoke a lot of weed and listen to songs that aren't the same ones they like best when they're alone. (They listen to Ella Fitzgerald, for example: they're aware that at their age it's still permissible to have discovered Ella Fitzgerald only recently.) They both nursed the fantasy of at least finishing Proust, of dragging things out over seven volumes and letting the last word (the word "Time") also be the last word that passed between them. Unfortunately, they only lasted a little over a month, reading at a rate of ten pages a day. They reached page 369, and from that point on, the book was left open.

*III.*

# Loans

First came Timothy, a rice-filled doll who looked vaguely like an elephant. Anita slept with Timothy, fought with Timothy, fed him, and even bathed him before giving him back to Emilia a week later. They were four years old at the time. Every other week the girls' parents got them together, and sometimes they spent both Saturday and Sunday playing hide-and-seek, talking in funny voices, and painting their faces with toothpaste.

Later it was clothes. Emilia liked Anita's maroon sweatshirt, and Anita asked for Emilia's Snoopy T-shirt in exchange, and thus began a steady trade that, over the years, grew chaotic. When they were eight there was a how-to book on origami that Anita returned to her friend with the edges a little beaten up. Between ten and twelve they took turns buying *Tú* magazine, and exchanged tapes of Miguel Bosé, Duran Duran, Álvaro Scaramelli, and Nadie.

When they were fourteen, Emilia kissed Anita on the

mouth, and Anita didn't know how to react. They didn't see each other for a few months after that. At seventeen Emilia kissed her again, and this time the kiss lasted a little longer. Anita laughed and told her she'd slap her if she did it again.

At seventeen Emilia enrolled at the University of Chile to study literature, because that was her lifelong dream. Of course, Anita knew studying literature was not Emilia's lifelong dream, but rather a whim directly related to her recent reading of Delmira Agustini. Anita's dream, on the other hand, was to lose a few pounds, which, needless to say, did not lead her to study nutrition or physical education. For the time being she enrolled in an intensive English class, and she ended up studying English intensively for several more years.

When they were twenty, Emilia and Anita moved in together. Anita had been living alone for six months, because her mother had started a new relationship and she deserved—as she told her daughter—the chance to start over from scratch. Starting from scratch meant starting without children and, most likely, remaining without them. But in this story Anita's mother and Anita don't matter, they're secondary characters. The one who matters is Emilia, who gladly accepted Anita's invitation to move in, enticed, in particular, by the prospect of being free to fuck Julio at her leisure.

Anita found out she was pregnant two months before her friend's relationship with Julio completely dissolved. The father—the *responsible party*, as some people said then—was in his last year as a law student at the Catholic University, a fact that Anita emphasized, probably because it made her slipup more seemly. Though they hadn't known each other long, Anita and the future lawyer decided to get married, and Emilia was a witness at the ceremony. During the party, while they danced to a cumbia, a friend of the groom's tried to kiss Emilia, but she turned her face away, arguing she didn't like that kind of music.

By twenty-six Anita was already the mother of two little girls, and her husband was of two minds about whether to buy a truck or give in to the vague temptation of a third child ("to shut down the factory," he said, in an attempt to be funny, and maybe he was, since people did tend to laugh at the comment). So that's how well they were doing.

Anita's husband was named Andrés, or Leonardo. Let's say his name was Andrés and not Leonardo. Let's say

Anita was awake and Andrés half-asleep and the two girls fast asleep on the night when Emilia unexpectedly dropped by to visit them.

It was almost eleven at night. Anita did her best to evenly distribute the little whiskey that was left in the bottle, and Andrés had to run out to buy some snacks at a nearby store. He came back with three small bags of potato chips.

Why didn't you buy a big bag?
Because they didn't have any big bags.
And it didn't occur to you, for example, to buy five small bags?
They didn't have five small bags. They only had three.

Emilia thought maybe it hadn't been such a good idea to drop in on her friend unannounced. While the spat lasted, she focused on a giant Mexican sombrero that dominated the room. She would have left, but she had come for an urgent reason: At school they thought she was married. In order to get a job as a Spanish teacher, she had said she was married. The problem was that there was a party the next night with her coworkers, and it was unavoidable that her husband go with her. After so many shirts and albums and books and even padded bras, it wouldn't be such a big deal for you to lend me your husband, said Emilia.

All her coworkers wanted to meet Miguel. And Andrés could perfectly well pass for Miguel. She had told them that Miguel was fat, dark, and friendly, and Andrés was, at least, very dark-skinned and very fat. Friendly he was not, that's what Emilia had thought from the first time she laid eyes on him, several years ago now. Anita was also fat, and beautiful, or at least as beautiful as a woman that fat can be, thought Emilia, a little enviously. Emilia herself was rather harsh-looking and very thin, while Anita was fat and pretty. Anita said she didn't see any problem with lending out her husband for a while.

As long as you give him back.
You can count on it.

They laughed hard, while Andrés tried to fish the last chip crumbs from his bag. As teenagers they had always been very careful when it came to guys. Before getting involved with anyone Emilia would call Anita, and vice versa, to ask the obligatory questions. Are you sure you don't like him? Positive, don't make it weird, man.

At first Andrés seemed reluctant, but he ended up agreeing. After all, the thing could turn out to be fun.

You know why rum and Coke is called a Cuba libre?

No, replied Emilia, a little tired and really wishing the party would end.

You really don't know? It's pretty obvious: rum is Cuba and Coca-Cola is the United States, freedom. Get it?

I heard something different.

What was it?

I used to know, but I forgot.

Andrés had already made several contributions along those lines, which was making it hard not to find him insufferable. Such an effort was he making to keep Emilia's coworkers from catching on to their lie that he'd even allowed himself to shush her. Apparently, Emilia said to herself then, it's normal for a husband to shush his wife. Andrés shushes Anita when he thinks she should be quiet. So there's nothing wrong with Miguel shushing his wife if he thinks she should be quiet. And since I am Miguel's wife, I have to be quiet.

And that's how Emilia spent the rest of the evening—silent. No one would doubt that she was married to Miguel now, nor would her colleagues be all that surprised by a marital crisis of, say, a couple of weeks, followed by a sudden but justified separation. And then, nothing more: no phone calls, no friends in common, nothing. It would be easy to kill Miguel. I cut that relationship off at the root, she imagined herself telling them.

Andrés parked the car and considered it necessary to wrap up the evening by telling Emilia that the party had been really fun, and he wouldn't mind at all if she wanted him to attend others. They're nice people, and that turquoise dress looks great on you.

The dress was teal, but she decided not to correct him. They were in front of Emilia's building, and it was still early. He was wasted, and she too had drunk her fair share, and maybe that's why suddenly it didn't seem so horrible for Andrés—for Miguel—to pause awhile between one word and another. But those thoughts were violently interrupted the moment she imagined her voluminous companion penetrating her. Gross, she thought, right at the moment Andrés got a little too close and placed his left hand on Emilia's right thigh.

She wanted to get out of the car, and he felt differently. She told him, You're drunk, and he replied that, no, it wasn't the alcohol, that for some time now he had seen her in a different light. It's hard to believe, but that's what he said: "I've seen you in a different light for some time now." He tried to kiss her, and she responded with a punch in the face. Blood flowed from Andrés's mouth, a lot of blood, a scandalous amount.

The two friends didn't see each other again for a long time after that incident. Anita never found out exactly what had happened, but she could imagine. At first she didn't like what she imagined, and later on she felt indifferent, since Andrés interested her less and less.

Neither truck nor third baby materialized. Instead there were two years of calculated silence and a separation that was pretty friendly, all things considered, and which, over time, led Andrés to think of himself as an excellent divorced dad. The girls stayed over at his house every other weekend, and they also spent the whole month of January with him in Maitencillo. One of those summers, Anita took the opportunity to visit Emilia. Her guilt-ridden mother had offered to pay for the trip several times, and although it was hard for Anita to be so far away from her daughters, she let curiosity win out.

She went to Madrid, but she didn't go for Madrid. She went to look for Emilia, whom she had totally lost track of. It hadn't been easy to chase down the address on Calle del Salitre and a phone number that, to Anita, seemed oddly long. When she landed in Barajas she almost dialed the number, but she held off, driven by a childish, atavistic fondness for surprises.

Madrid wasn't beautiful, at least not to Anita, to the Anita who that morning had to maneuver out of the Metro around a group of Moroccans who seemed to be plotting something. They were actually Ecuadoreans and Colombians, but Anita, who had never met a Moroccan in her life, thought of them as Moroccan, since she remembered seeing a man on TV recently who said that Moroccans were Spain's biggest problem. Madrid struck her as an intimidating, hostile city; in fact, it was hard to choose someone who looked trustworthy enough to ask for directions to the address she had written down. There were several cryptic conversations after leaving the Metro and before she was finally face-to-face with Emilia.

You started wearing black again, was the first thing Anita said. But the first thing she said was not the first thing she thought. Anita thought a lot of things when she saw Emilia: she thought, You look bad, You're depressed, You look like a junkie. She realized maybe she shouldn't have made this trip. She looked closely at

Emilia's eyebrows, Emilia's eyes. She studied the place with contempt: a cramped apartment in frank disarray, discordant and overcrowded. She thought, or rather felt, that she didn't want to hear what Emilia was going to tell her, that she wanted to avoid having to know what in any case she seemed condemned to find out. I don't want to know why there's so much shit in this neighborhood, why you came to live in this neighborhood full of shit, full of cagey eyes, weird kids, fat women lugging shopping bags, and fat women not lugging any bags but walking very slowly nonetheless. She looked closely, again, at Emilia's eyebrows. She decided it was better to keep quiet about Emilia's eyebrows.

You started wearing black again, Emilia.
Anita, you haven't changed.

Emilia did say the first thing she thought: You haven't changed. You're the same, you're still like that, how you are. And I'm still like this, I've always been this way, and maybe now I'm going to tell you that in Madrid I've become even more like this, completely this.

Well aware of her friend's prejudices, Emilia informed Anita that the two men she lived with were poor and gay.

Gays in Madrid dress really well, she said, but these two who live with me, unfortunately, are dirt-poor. Anita didn't want to stay with Emilia. They went out together to find a cheap hostel, and it could be said that they talked for a long time, though maybe not; it would be incorrect to say that they talked the way they used to, because where there had been trust before, now what united them was a feeling of discomfort, of guilty familiarity, of shame and emptiness. Near the end of the day, after making some urgent mental calculations, Anita took out forty thousand pesetas, which was almost all the money she had with her. She gave it to Emilia, who, far from protesting, smiled with real gratitude. Anita knew that smile from before, and it reunited them for a couple of seconds before leaving them alone again, face-to-face, one of them wishing that for the rest of the week the tourist would stick to museums, Zara shops, and syrupy pancakes, and the other promising herself that she wasn't going to think any more about how Emilia would use her forty thousand pesetas.

*IV.*

# Leftovers

Gazmuri doesn't matter; Julio is the one who matters. Gazmuri has published six or seven novels that together comprise a series on Chile's recent history. Almost no one has understood them, except maybe Julio, who has read and reread them several times.

How is it that Gazmuri and Julio come together?

It would be excessive to say that they come together.

But yes: One Saturday in January, Gazmuri waits for Julio in a café in Providencia. He has just finished a new novel: five Colón notebooks filled with handwritten text. Usually his wife takes care of transcribing his notebooks, but this time she doesn't want to, she's tired. She's tired of Gazmuri, it's been weeks since she spoke to him, and that's why Gazmuri looks exhausted and unkempt. But Gazmuri's wife isn't important, Gazmuri himself isn't all that important. So, the old man called his friend Natalia, and his friend Natalia said she was too busy to transcribe the novel, but she recommended Julio.

———

Do you write by hand? No one writes by hand these days, observes Gazmuri, not waiting for Julio to answer. But Julio does answer, he says no, he almost always uses the computer.

Gazmuri: Then you don't know what I'm talking about, you don't know the momentum. There's a momentum that comes from writing on paper, from the sound of the pen. A strange equilibrium between elbow, hand, and pen.

Julio talks, but there's no hearing what he says. Some-one needs to turn his volume up. But Gazmuri's voice booms, hoarse and intense; it's working fine:

Do you write novels, those forty-page novels with short chapters that are so in fashion?

Julio: No. And he adds, just to say something: Do you think I should write novels?

What a question. I'm not telling you what to do, I don't recommend anything to anyone. You think I called this meeting so I could give you advice?

It's hard to talk to Gazmuri, thinks Julio. Hard, but pleasant. Before long Gazmuri is straight-up talking to himself. He talks about various political and literary conspiracies, and he emphasizes, especially, one idea: You have to protect yourself from the mortuary makeup artists. I'm sure *you* would just love to slap some makeup on me. Young people like you get close to old people because you like that we're old. Being young is a disadvantage, not a characteristic. You should know that. When I was young I felt I was at a disadvantage, and I do now too. Being old is also a disadvantage. Because we old folks are weak and we need more than just praise from young people; ultimately, we need their blood. An old person needs a lot of blood, whether or not he writes novels. And you have a lot of blood. Maybe the only thing you have to spare, now that I get a good look at you, is blood.

Julio doesn't know how to respond. He's saved by a long peal of laughter from Gazmuri, a laugh that implies that at least some of what he's just said is a joke. And Julio laughs with him; he's enjoying being there, playing a secondary character. He wants, as long as possible, to stay in that role, but to stay in the role he surely has to say something, something that will make him relevant. A joke, for example. But he can't think of a joke. He says nothing. It's Gazmuri who says:

Something very important in the novel you're going to transcribe happens on this corner. That's why I wanted to meet here. Toward the end of the novel, something important happens right on this corner; this is an important corner. By the way, how much do you plan to charge me?

Julio: A hundred thousand pesos?

Really, Julio would be willing to work for free, though he doesn't exactly have money to spare. To him it's a privilege to drink coffee and smoke cigarettes with Gazmuri. He says a hundred thousand the way he said hello earlier, mechanically. And he goes on listening, he follows a little behind Gazmuri, agrees unquestioningly, though he would rather just listen to everything, absorb information, to be, now, full of information:

Let's just say this is my most personal novel. It's very different from the ones that came before. I'll summarize it a little: A guy finds out that a girlfriend from his youth is dead. He turns on the radio like he does every morning, and he hears the woman's name in an obituary. First name, middle name, and two last names. That's how it all begins.

All what?

Everything, absolutely everything. I'll call you, then, as soon as I make a decision.

But what else happens?

Nothing. Same thing as always. Everything goes to shit. I'll call you, then, as soon as I decide.

Julio walks to his apartment visibly confused. Maybe it was a mistake to ask for a hundred thousand pesos, but then again, he's not sure that amount means much to a man like Gazmuri. Julio does need the money, of course. Twice a week he gives Latin lessons to the daughter of a right-wing intellectual. That, plus what's left of the balance on a credit card his father gave him, is his entire disposable income.

He lives in a garden apartment in a building in Plaza Italia. When the heat stupefies him, he kills time watching people's shoes out the window. That day, right before turning his key, he realizes that his neighbor María is just getting home. He sees her shoes, her sandals. And he waits, calculates the number of steps and the greeting to the doorman, until he hears her approaching, and then he focuses on opening the door: he pretends he can't find the right key, even though there are only two on his key chain. It's like neither of them fits, he says very loudly, as he looks sideways and just catches a glimpse of her.

He sees her long white hair, which makes her face look darker than it really is. At some point they had a conversation about Severo Sarduy. She isn't much of a reader, but she's very well-versed in the work of Severo Sarduy. She's forty or forty-five years old, lives alone, and reads Severo Sarduy: and that's why—because two plus two equals four—Julio thinks that María is a lesbian. Julio likes Severo Sarduy too, his essays in particular, so he always has something to talk about with gays and lesbians.

That day, in a dress she rarely wears, María looks less somber than usual. Julio is about to compliment it, but he stops himself, thinking maybe she doesn't like those kinds of comments. Wanting to forget about his interview with Gazmuri, he invites her in for coffee. They talk about Sarduy, about *Cobra* and *Cocuyo*, about *Big Bang* and *Written on a Body*. But they also—and this is new—talk about other neighbors, about politics, odd salads, tooth whiteners, vitamin supplements, and about a walnut sauce she wants Julio to try one day. The moment arrives when they run out of topics and it seems inevitable that they will both get back to work. María is an English teacher, but she also works at home, translating software manuals and stereo instructions. He tells her that he's just gotten a good job, an interesting job, with Gazmuri, the novelist.

I've never read him, but I've heard he's good. I have a brother in Barcelona who knows him. They were in exile there at the same time, I think.

And Julio: I'm starting my job with Gazmuri tomorrow. He needs someone to transcribe his new novel, because he writes by hand and doesn't like computers.

What's the novel called?

He wants us to talk about the title, he wants to discuss it. A man finds out from the radio that an old flame from his youth has died. That's how everything starts, absolutely everything.

And what happens then?

He never forgot her, she was his great love. When they were young they took care of a plant.

A plant? A bonsai?

Right, a bonsai. They decided to buy a bonsai to symbolize the great love that bound them. Then everything went to shit, but he never forgot her. He lived his life, had children, separated, but he never forgot her. One day he finds out she's dead. Then he decides to do something to honor her. I still don't know what he does.

Two bottles of wine and then sex. Her fine lines are suddenly more visible, in spite of the dimly lit room. Julio's movements are belated; María, though, gets a little ahead of the script, sensing Julio's hesitation. His tremor subsides a little, becomes more of a rhythmic and even judicious shudder that naturally leads toward the pelvic game.

For a moment Julio lingers over María's white hair: it looks like a fine but frayed fabric, immensely fragile. A fabric that must be caressed with care and love. But it's hard to caress with care and love: Julio chooses instead to move down her torso and lift her dress. She runs her fingers over his ears, feels the shape of his nose, smooths his sideburns. He thinks that he should suck not what a man would suck, but what the woman she must be picturing would suck. But María interrupts Julio's thoughts: I want you in me right now, she tells him.

At eight in the morning the phone rings. Miss Silvia from Planeta says she'll charge me forty thousand pesos for the transcription, says Gazmuri. Sorry.

Gazmuri's curtness disconcerts him. It's eight in the

morning on a Sunday, the phone has just woken him up, the lesbian or non-lesbian or ex-lesbian sleeping beside him is starting to stir. Gazmuri has turned him down for the job, and Miss Silvia, from Planeta, for forty thousand pesos, is going to do it. Though María isn't even awake enough to ask who called or what time it is, Julio replies:

It was Gazmuri, he must be an early riser, or else he's really anxious. He called to confirm that we'll start on *Bonsai* this afternoon. That's what the novel will be called: *Bonsai*.

What follows is something like a romance. A romance that lasts less than a year, until she leaves for Madrid. María moves to Madrid because she has to go, but above all because she has no reason to stay. All the ladies leave you for Madrid, Julio's crass friends would have joked, except Julio doesn't have any crass friends, he's always shielded himself from crass friendships. Anyway, this story isn't so interested in María. This story is interested in Julio:

He never forgot her, says Julio. He lived his life, had kids and everything, got separated, but he didn't forget her. She was a translator, same as you, but of Japanese. The two of them met when they were both studying Japanese, many years ago. When she dies, he thinks that the best way to remember her is by growing another bonsai.

So he buys a bonsai?

No, this time he doesn't buy it, he makes it. He gets manuals, consults experts, plants the seeds. He goes kind of crazy.

María says it's a weird story.

Yeah, it's just that Gazmuri writes really well. The way I'm telling it to you it seems like a weird story, melodramatic, maybe. But I'm sure Gazmuri knows how to shape it just right.

The first imaginary meeting with Gazmuri takes place that same Sunday. Julio buys four Colón notebooks and spends the afternoon writing on a bench in Forestal Park. He writes frenetically, in a handwriting that isn't his. He keeps working on *Bonsai* that night, and by Monday morning he has finished the first notebook of the novel. He smudges a few paragraphs, spills coffee on the pages, and even scatters some ashes over the manuscript.

To María: It's the greatest test for a writer. Practically nothing happens in *Bonsai*. There's enough plot for a two-page story, and maybe not even a good one.

What are their names?

The characters'? Gazmuri didn't give them names. He says it's better that way, and I agree: they're He and She, John and Jane Doe, they don't have names and they might not have faces either. The protagonist is a king or a beggar, it doesn't matter. A king or a beggar who lets go of the only woman he's ever really loved.

And he learned to speak Japanese?

They met in a Japanese class. But I actually don't know yet, I think that's in the second notebook.

Over the following months Julio spends his mornings faking Gazmuri's handwriting, and his afternoons in front of the computer transcribing a novel that could be his own or someone else's, he no longer knows. But he is determined to finish, to finish imagining it, at least. He thinks that the final text is the perfect going-away present for María, the only possible gift. And that's what he does, he finishes the manuscript and gives it to María.

During the days after she leaves, Julio starts several urgent emails that nevertheless stay stuck in his drafts folder for weeks. Finally, he decides to send her the following:

I've thought a lot about you. I'm sorry, I didn't have time to write before now. I hope you made it there OK.

Gazmuri wants us to keep working together, although he hasn't really told me on what. I guess

another novel. The truth is I don't know if I want
to keep putting up with his indecisiveness, his
cough, his scratchy voice, his theories. I haven't
gone back to giving Latin lessons. There's not
much more to tell you. The book launch is next
week. At the last minute Gazmuri decided to call it
*Leftovers*. I don't think it's a very good title, so I'm
a little mad at him, but, in the end, he's the author.

Hugs, J

Fearful and confused, Julio heads to the National Library to witness the launch of *Leftovers*, Gazmuri's real novel. From the back of the hall he can see the author, who nods once in a while to show he agrees with the observations made by Ebensperger, the critic who is presenting the book. The critic moves his hands insistently to demonstrate that he is truly interested in the novel. The editor, for her part, blatantly scans the audience for their reactions.

Julio only half listens to the presentation: Dr. Ebensperger alludes to literary courage and artistic intransigence; he recalls, in passing, a book by Rilke; he employs an idea of Walter Benjamin's (though doesn't give credit for it); and he invokes a poem by Enrique Lihn (whom he

just calls Enrique) that, according to him, perfectly en-
capsulates the conflict in *Leftovers*: "A gravely ill patient /
masturbates to show signs of life."


Before the editor starts to speak, Julio leaves the hall
and walks toward Providencia. Half an hour later, almost
without realizing it, he has reached the café where he met
Gazmuri. He decides to stay there, waiting for something
important to happen. Meanwhile, he smokes. He drinks
coffee and smokes.

*V.*

# Two Drawings

Someone died going the wrong way,
holding up traffic.

—CHICO BUARQUE

The end of this story should give us hope, but it does not.

One particularly long day, Julio decides to start two drawings. The first is of a woman who is María but also Emilia: Emilia's dark, almost black eyes, and María's white hair; María's ass, Emilia's thighs, María's feet; the back of a right-wing intellectual's daughter; Emilia's cheeks, María's nose, María's lips; Emilia's torso and small breasts; Emilia's pubis.

The second drawing is easier in theory, but it turns out to be very difficult for Julio, who spends several weeks sketching until he gets the image he wanted:

It's a tree on the edge.

—————

Julio hangs both images on the bathroom mirror as if they were freshly developed photographs. And there they remain, covering the mirror's surface completely. Julio doesn't dare name the woman he has drawn. He calls her She. His very own She, of course. And he invents a story for her, a story that he doesn't write, that he doesn't bother to write.

Since his father and mother refuse to give him money, Julio decides to set himself up as a vendor on a corner of Plaza Italia. Business is good: in just one week he sells nearly half his books. He gets especially good prices for the poetry of Octavio Paz (*The Best of Octavio Paz*) and Ungaretti (*Life of a Man*), and for an old edition of Neruda's *Complete Works*. He also parts with a dictionary of quotations published by Espasa-Calpe, an essay on Gogol by Claudio Giaconi, a couple of novels by Cristina Peri Rossi that he's never read, and, finally, *Alhué* by González Vera and *Fermina Márquez* by Valery Larbaud, two novels he *has* read, many times, but that he is never going to read again.

He uses some of the money from the sales to read up on bonsai. He buys manuals and specialized magazines, which he pores over with methodical eagerness. One of the manuals, perhaps the least useful of them but the one most suited to an amateur, starts like this:

> *A bonsai is an artistic replica of a tree in minia-*
> *ture. It consists of two elements: the living tree*
> *and the container. The two elements must be in*
> *harmony, and the selection of the right pot for a*
> *tree is almost an art form in itself. The plant can*
> *be a climbing vine, a shrub, or a tree, but it is*
> *always referred to as a tree. The container is nor-*
> *mally a flowerpot or interesting piece of rock. A*
> *bonsai is never called a bonsai tree. The word al-*
> *ready includes the living element. Once out of the*
> *container, the tree is no longer a bonsai.*

Julio memorizes the definition, because he likes the part about how a rock can be considered interesting, and be-cause the paragraph's various specifications seem oppor-tune. "The selection of the right pot for a tree is almost an art form in itself," he thinks, and repeats, until he becomes convinced that those words hold essential information. He is ashamed, then, of *Bonsai*, his improvised novel, his unnecessary novel, whose protagonist doesn't even know that the choice of a container is an art form in itself, that a bonsai isn't a bonsai tree because the word already includes the living element.

Tending a bonsai is like writing, thinks Julio. Writing is like tending a bonsai, Julio thinks.

In the mornings he searches, reluctantly, for a stable job. He comes home at midafternoon and barely takes the time to eat before returning to the manuals: he tries to be as systematic as possible, consumed as he is by a glimmer of fulfillment. He reads until sleep overcomes him. He reads about the most common diseases among bonsai, about how to spray the leaves, about pruning, about the use of wire. He buys, at last, seeds and tools.

And he does it. He grows a bonsai.

It's a woman, a young woman.

That's all that María ever knows about Emilia. The dead person is a dead woman—a young woman, says someone behind her. A young woman has thrown herself in front of a train in Antón Martín. For a moment María considers approaching the place where it happened, but immediately suppresses the urge. She emerges from the Metro thinking about the imagined face of the young woman who has just committed suicide. She thinks about herself, once upon a time, less sad but more desperate than she is now. She thinks about a house in Chile, in Santiago de Chile, and its garden. A garden without flowers and without trees that nevertheless has the right, she thinks, to be called a garden, because it *is* a garden, indisputably. She remembers that song by Violeta Parra: "The flowers of my garden / must be my caretakers." She walks toward the Fuentetaja bookstore, because that afternoon she's meeting a date there. The name of her date doesn't matter, except that on the way there her thoughts turn, suddenly, to him, to the bookstore and the hookers on Calle Montera and also to other hookers on other streets that are beside the point, and then to a movie, the title of a movie she saw five or six years ago. That's how she starts to be distracted from Emilia's story, from this story. María disappears on the way to the Fuentetaja bookstore. She walks away from Emilia's body and starts to disappear from this story forever.

She's gone.

Now there's only Emilia, alone, holding up the operation of the Metro.

Very far from Emilia's cadaver, there, here, in Santiago de Chile, Anita listens to yet another of her mother's now-habitual confessions about her marital problems, which seem endless and which Anita analyzes with angry commiseration, as if they were her own problems, in a way relieved they are not actually her problems.

Andrés, on the other hand, is nervous: He has a medical checkup in ten minutes, and although there isn't the slightest sign of illness, it suddenly seems clear to him that he will receive terrible news in the coming days. He thinks, then, about his daughters, and about Anita and someone else, some other woman he always remembers, even when it doesn't seem appropriate to remember anyone. Just then he sees an old man on his way out, walking with a satisfied expression, calculating his steps, patting his pockets in search of cigarettes or coins. Andrés realizes it's his turn, that now the moment has come for the routine blood tests, then the routine X-rays, and after that, maybe, the routine CAT scan. The old man who has just left the doctor's office is Gazmuri. They haven't greeted each other, they don't know each other, and they will never meet. Gazmuri is happy, since he hasn't died: he leaves the clinic thinking about how he hasn't died, how there are few things in life as pleasant as knowing one has not died. Once again, he thinks, I've just scraped by.

On the first night in the world with Emilia dead, Julio sleeps badly, but by then he is used to his anxiety keeping him up at night. For months now he's been waiting for the moment when the bonsai will start to take on its perfect shape, the serene and noble shape he has planned for it.

The tree follows the course set by the wire. Sometime in the coming years, Julio figures, it will look, finally, like the drawing. The four or five times he wakes up that night, he looks in on the bonsai. In between, he dreams about something like a desert or a beach, a place with sand, where three people stare up toward the sun or the sky, as if they were on vacation or as if they had died unexpectedly while sunbathing. Suddenly, a purple bear appears. A very large bear that slowly lumbers toward the bodies, and just as slowly starts to walk around them, until it makes a full circle.

I want to finish Julio's story, but Julio's story doesn't end, that's the problem.

Julio's story doesn't end, or else it ends like this:

Julio doesn't find out about Emilia's suicide until a year or a year and a half later. He hears the news from Andrés, who has gone with Anita and the girls to a children's book fair at Bustamante Park. And there, at the Recrea Editions stand, is Julio, working as a vendor—a badly paid but very easy job. Julio seems happy, because it's the last day of the fair, meaning that tomorrow he can go back to tending his bonsai. The encounter with Anita is muddled: At first Julio doesn't recognize her, but Anita thinks he's pretending, that he does recognize her but is displeased to see her. She clarifies her identity with some annoyance, and, in passing, mentions that she's been separated for several years from Andrés, whom Julio met briefly during the final days or pages of his relationship with Emilia. Clumsily, to make conversation, Julio asks for details, tries to understand why, if they're separated, they are together now, enacting a wholesome family outing. But neither Anita nor Andrés has a good answer to Julio's rude questions.

It's only as they're saying goodbye that Julio asks the question he should have asked from the beginning. Anita looks at him nervously and doesn't answer. She takes the girls to buy candy apples. It's Andrés who stays, who badly summarizes a very long story that no one knows well, a common story whose only particularity is that no one knows how to tell it well. Andrés says, then, that Emilia had an accident, and when Julio doesn't react, doesn't ask any questions, Andrés gets more specific: Emilia is dead. She jumped in front of a train or something, I don't really know. She'd gotten into drugs, supposedly, although not really, I don't think. She died, they buried her in Madrid, that much I know.

An hour later Julio receives his pay: three ten-thousand-peso bills that he had planned to live on for at least the next two weeks. Instead of walking to his apartment, he hails a taxi and asks the driver to drive thirty thousand pesos. He repeats it, explains, and even gives the money to the driver up front: go any direction, go in circles, diagonally, doesn't matter, I'll get out once the meter hits thirty thousand.

It's a long ride, without music, from Providencia to Las Rejas, and then, on the way back, Estación Central, Avenida Matta, Avenida Grecia, Tobalaba, Providencia, Bellavista. During the ride, Julio doesn't answer any of the questions the taxi driver asks him. He doesn't even hear them.

Read on for a selection from
Alejandro Zambra's forthcoming
novel, *The Private Lives of Trees*,
translated by Megan McDowell

J ulián lulls the little girl to sleep with "The Private Lives of Trees," a series of stories he makes up to tell her at bedtime. The protagonists are a poplar tree and a baobab who, at night, when no one is watching, talk about photosynthesis, squirrels, or the many advantages of being trees and not people or animals, or, as they put it, stupid hunks of cement.

Daniela is not his daughter, but it is hard for him not to think of her that way. It's been three years since Julián joined the family. He was the one who came to them—Verónica and Daniela were already there. He married Verónica, and in some ways also Daniela, who was hesitant at first, but little by little began to accept her new life: Julián is uglier than my dad, but he's nice, she would say to her friends, who nodded with surprising seriousness, even solemnity, as if they somehow just knew that Julián's arrival was not an accident. As the months passed this stepfather even earned a place in the drawings Daniela made at school. There's one in particular that Julián always keeps out: the three of them are at the beach, Daniela and Verónica are making sand cakes, and he is dressed in jeans and a shirt, reading and smoking under a perfectly round and yellow sun.

Julián is uglier than Daniela's father, but he's also younger; he works more and makes less money, smokes more and drinks less; he exercises less—doesn't, in fact, exercise at all—and he knows more about trees than about countries. He is lighter-skinned and less simple and more confused than Fernando—Fernando, because that is Daniela's father's name. He must have a name, even if he isn't, exactly, Julián's enemy, or anyone else's. Really, there is no enemy here. That is precisely the problem: in this story there are no enemies. Verónica has no enemies, Julián has no enemies, Fernando has no enemies, and Daniela, except for an impish little classmate who spends all his time making faces at her, has no enemies either.

. . .

Sometimes Fernando is a blot on Daniela's life, but who isn't, at times, a blot on someone else's life.

Julián is Fernando without the blot, but sometimes Fernando is Julián without the blot.

And Verónica, who is:

For now Verónica is someone who is not home, who isn't back yet from her drawing class. Verónica is someone who is lightly missing from the blue room—the blue room is Daniela's bedroom, and the white room is Verónica and Julián's.

There is, in addition, a green bedroom, which they call the guest room mostly in jest, since it wouldn't be easy to sleep in that mess of books, folders, and paintbrushes. The big trunk where they stored their summer clothes a few months back is set up as an uncomfortable sofa.

The final hours of a normal day have settled into an impeccable routine: Julián and Verónica leave the blue room when Daniela falls asleep, and then, in the guest room, Verónica draws and Julián reads. Every once in a while she interrupts him or he interrupts her, and these mutual interferences constitute dialogues, light conversations or sometimes important, decisive ones. Later they move to the white room, where they watch TV or make love or start to argue—nothing serious, nothing that can't be fixed immediately, before the movie is over or when one of them gives up, wanting to sleep or have sex. The usual end to those fights is a fast and silent screw, or maybe a long one replete with soft laughter and moans. Then come five or six hours of sleep. And then the next day begins.

But this is not a normal night, at least not yet. It's still not completely certain that there will be a next day, since Verónica isn't back yet from her drawing class. When she returns, the novel will end. But as long as she is not back, the book will continue. The book goes on until she returns, or until Julián is sure that she isn't going to come back. For now, Verónica is missing from the blue room, where Julián lulls the little girl to sleep with a story about the private lives of trees.

Right now, sheltered in the solitude of the park, the trees are commenting on the bad luck of an oak, in whose bark two people have carved their names as a symbol of their friendship. No one has the right to give you a tattoo without your consent, says the poplar, and the baobab is even more emphatic: The oak tree has been the victim of a deplorable act of vandalism. Those people deserve to be punished. I shall not rest until they get the punishment they deserve. I will travel the earth, sky, and sea to hunt them down.

Daniela laughs hard, without the least sign of sleepiness. And she urgently, anxiously asks the inevitable questions, never just one, always at least two or three: What's vandalism, Julián? Can I have some lemonade, with three spoonfuls of sugar? Did you and my mom ever carve your names into a tree as a symbol of your friendship?

Julián answers patiently, trying to respect the order of the questions: Vandalism is what vandals do; vandals are people who do damage just for the joy of doing damage. And yes, you can have some lemonade. And no, your mom and I never carved our names into the bark of a tree.

In the beginning, Verónica and Julián's story was not a love story. In fact, they met for more commercial reasons. At that time he was living through the last gasps of a prolonged relationship with Karla, a distant and sullen woman who was on the verge of becoming his enemy. There was, for them, no great reason to celebrate, but all the same Julián called up Verónica, a pastry chef, at the recommendation of a colleague, and ordered a tres leches cake that ended up brightening Karla's birthday significantly. When Julián went to Verónica's apartment—the same one they now live in—to pick up the cake, he saw a dark, thin woman with long, straight hair and brown eyes. A Chilean woman, in other words, one with nervous gestures, serious and happy at the same time—a beautiful woman, who had a daughter and maybe also a husband. As he waited in the living room for Verónica to finish packing up the cake, Julián caught a glimpse of the white face of a very little girl. Then there was a short exchange between Daniela and her mother, a sharp but congenial exchange, commonplace, perhaps a back-and-forth about brushing teeth.

It would be imprecise to say that Julián was captivated by Verónica that day. The truth is that there were three or four seconds of awkwardness; that is, Julián should have left the apartment three or four seconds sooner, and if he didn't it was

5

because it seemed pleasant to stay looking three or four seconds longer at Verónica's clear, dark face.

Julián finishes his tale, satisfied with the story he has told, but Daniela is not asleep; on the contrary, she seems alert, ready to keep the conversation going. Employing a delicate detour, the girl starts telling him about school until, out of nowhere, she confesses a desire to have blue hair. He smiles, thinking it a metaphorical wish, like the dream of flying or time travel. But she's speaking seriously: Two girls and even a boy in my class have dyed their hair. I want a blue streak, at least—well, I don't know if I want blue or red, I can't decide, she says, as if the decision were hers to make. This is a new subject: Julián realizes the girl has already talked about it with her mother in the afternoon, and now she is seeking her stepfather's approval. And the stepfather fumblingly tries out a position in the game: You're only eight years old, why would you want to ruin your hair so young? he asks, and then improvises an evasive family story that somehow or other proves that dyeing one's hair is madness. The conversation continues until, a bit indignant, Daniela begins to yawn.

He sees Daniela sleeping, and he imagines himself, at eight years old, sleeping. It's a reflex: he sees a blind man and imagines himself blind; he reads a good poem and pictures himself writing it, or reading it aloud, to nobody, encouraged by the dark sound of the words. Julián simply observes these images, receives them, and then forgets them. Perhaps he has always merely chased images: he hasn't made decisions, hasn't won or lost, but has just let himself be drawn in by certain images, and then followed them, without fear or courage, until he caught or extinguished them.

Stretched out on the bed in the white room, Julián lights a cigarette, the last one of the day, the next to last, or perhaps the first one of an immensely long night, during which he is fated to go over the pluses and minuses of a past that is, frankly, blurry. For now, life is a chaos that seems to be resolved: he has been welcomed into a new intimacy, into a world where his role is to be something like a father to Daniela, the sleeping little girl, and a husband to Verónica, the woman who isn't back, not yet, from her drawing class. From here the story dissipates, and there is almost no way to continue it. For now, though, Julián achieves a sort of distance from which to watch, attentively, with legitimate interest, the rerun of an old match between Inter and Reggina. It's clear that Inter will score their goal any minute now, and Julián doesn't want to miss it, not for anything.

Veronica was in her second of year studying for an art degree when Daniela arrived and threw everything off course.

Anticipating the pain was her way of experiencing it—a young pain that grew and shrank and sometimes, during certain especially warm hours, tended to disappear. She decided to keep the news to herself during the first weeks of pregnancy; she didn't even tell Fernando or her best girlfriend, though she didn't have a best friend, not really. That is, she had lots of girlfriends and they always turned to her for advice, but she never fully reciprocated their confidence. That time of silence was one last luxury Verónica could give herself, an addendum of privacy, a space of doubtful calm in which to assemble her decisions. I don't want to be a pregnant student. I don't want to be a student mother, she thought. She definitely did not want to find herself in a few months time, wrapped in a very wide and very flowered dress, explaining to the professor that she hadn't been able to study for the test, or later, two years on, leaving the baby in the librarians' care. She felt panic when she imagined those librarians and their besotted faces when she converted them, suddenly, into the faithful guardians of other people's children.

During that time she went to dozens of art galleries, boldly interrogated her professors, and lost many hours letting herself be courted by upper-level art students, who, predictably, turned out to be insufferable rich kids—rich kids claiming to be bad boys who nevertheless found success faster than their civil engineer brothers or their educational psychologist sisters.

Sooner rather than later, Verónica found the resentment she was looking for: this was not a world she wanted to be part of—this wasn't a world that she *could* be part of, not even close. From then on, every time she was devastated by a dark thought about her abandoned vocation, she called up the counterexamples she had collected. Instead of thinking about the healthy disdain some of her professors felt toward artistic fads, she remembered the classes of two or three of those charlatans who always seem to find their way into art departments. And instead of thinking about the honest, true works some of her classmates created, she decided to recall the naive galleries where acquiescent and well-connected students showed off their discoveries.

Those young artists imitated the language of the academy to perfection, eagerly filling out endless forms for government grants. But the money soon ran out, and the young artists had to resign themselves to teaching classes for amateurs, like the ones Verónica attends in the inhospitable event hall of a nearby municipal building. In the mornings, Verónica bakes sponge cakes and answers the phone. In the afternoons, she delivers orders and attends class, where she sometimes gets bored and other times enjoys herself: she works with agility and discipline, finally comfortable with her amateur status. She should have been back from her drawing class over an hour ago—she must be on her way, thinks Julián as he watches TV. Then, in the eighty-eighth minute and against all odds, Reggina scores a goal. And that's how the game ends: Inter 0, Reggina 1.

Last week, Julián turned thirty years old. The party was a bit odd, marred by the guest of honor's glumness. In the same way that some women subtract years from their real age, he sometimes needs to add a few on, to look at the past with a whimsical tinge of bitterness. Lately he has started to think he should have been a dentist or geologist or meteorologist. For now, his actual job seems strange: teacher. But his true calling, he thinks now, is to have dandruff. He imagines himself answering that way:

"What's your job?"

"I have dandruff."

———

He's exaggerating, no doubt about it. No one can live without a little exaggeration. If there are in fact stages in Julián's life, they would have to be expressed according to an exaggeration index. He exaggerated very little, almost never, up until he was ten years old. From ten to seventeen his pretensions increased steadily, and from eighteen onward he was an expert in the most varied forms of exaggeration. Since he's been with Verónica, his exaggeration has been decreasing consistently, notwithstanding the occasional, instinctive relapse.

Julián is a literature professor at four universities in Santiago. He would have liked to stick to one specialty, but the law of supply and demand has forced him to be flexible: he teaches classes in US literature and Latin American literature and even Italian poetry, in spite of the fact that he does not speak Italian. He has read, and closely, translations of Ungaretti, Montale, Pavese, and Pasolini, as well as more recent poets, like Patrizia Cavalli and Valerio Magrelli, but in no way could he be considered an expert in Italian poetry. In any case, teaching classes in Italian poetry without knowing Italian is not terribly unusual in Chile, as Santiago is full of English teachers who don't know English, dentists who can hardly pull a tooth, overweight personal trainers, and yoga teachers who wouldn't be able to face their classes without a generous dose of antidepressants. Julián tends to emerge unscathed from his pedagogical adventures.

He always salvages any situation by camouflaging some quotation from Walter Benjamin, Borges, or Nicanor Parra.

He is a professor, and a writer on Sundays. There are weeks when he works as much as he possibly can, obsessively, as if trying to meet a deadline. He calls that his "busy season." Normally, in the off-season, he defers his literary ambitions until Sunday, the way other men devote their Sundays to gardening or carpentry or alcoholism.

He has just finished a very short book that nevertheless took several years to write. First he collected material: he wrote almost three hundred pages, but then gradually reversed course, discarding more and more passages, as if instead of adding stories he wanted to subtract or erase them. The result was meager: an emaciated sheaf of forty-seven pages that he insists on calling a novel. Although earlier today he'd decided to let the book rest for a few weeks, he has now turned off the TV and begun, again, to read the manuscript.

. . .

Now he reads, he is reading: he tries to pretend he doesn't know the story, and at times he achieves the illusion—he lets himself be carried along, innocently, shyly, convincing himself that he's reading someone else's text. One misplaced comma or jarring word, though, and he snaps back to reality; he is then, once again, an *author*, the author of something, a kind of self-policeman who punishes his own mistakes, his excesses and inhibitions. He reads standing up, walking around the room: he should sit or lie down, but he stays on his feet, back straight, and he avoids the lamp, as if he's afraid that brighter light would reveal fresh mistakes in the manuscript.

The first image is of a young man tending a bonsai. If someone were to ask him for a summary of his book, he would probably respond that it was about a young man tending a bonsai. Maybe he wouldn't say a young man, maybe he would merely say that the protagonist is not exactly a boy or a mature adult or an old man. One night, several years ago now, he mentioned the image to his friends Sergio and Bernardita: a man shut in with his bonsai, tending it, moved by the possibility of a real work of art. A few days later, as a joke, they gave him a tiny elm. So you'll write your book, they told him.

In those days Julián lived alone, or more or less alone; that is, he lived with Karla, that strange woman who'd been on the verge of becoming his enemy. Back then Karla was almost never home, and she especially made sure to never be home when he got back from work. After making a cup of tea with amaretto—this seems repugnant to him now, but in those days he had a passion for tea with amaretto—Julián took care of his tree. He didn't just water it and prune it when necessary: he sat watching it for hours, waiting, perhaps, for it to move, the same way some children will lie motionless in bed at night, hoping to feel themselves grow.

Only after watching over his bonsai's growth for at least an hour would Julián sit down to write. There were inspired nights when he filled pages and pages with a sudden burst of confidence. There were other, less productive nights when he couldn't get past the first paragraph. He got stuck there looking at the screen, distracted and anxious, as if hoping the book would write itself. He lived on the second floor of a building across from Plaza Ñuñoa; the first floor was a bar from which issued a confusion of voices and the constant pulse of techno music. He liked to work with that music in the background, though he got hopelessly distracted when some particularly comic or sordid conversation reached his ears. He remembers, especially, the sour voice of an older woman who would talk about her father's death to anyone who would listen, and the panic of a teenager who, one early morning in winter, swore he would never screw without a condom again. More than once, he thought it would be worthwhile to write down what he heard, to record those conversations; he imagined a sea of words traveling from the ground to the window and from the window to his ear, to his hand, to his book. There would surely be more life in those accidental pages than in the book he was writing. But instead of being content with the stories that destiny put at his disposal, Julián forged ahead with his fixed idea of the bonsai.

## CHILEAN POET

### A Novel

When Gonzalo reunites with his first love, Carla, they form a stepfamily—though no such word exists in their language—with her son, Vicente. Though ambition ultimately pulls the lovers apart, Vicente still inherits his ex-stepfather's love of poetry and encourages Pru, an American journalist, to chronicle the endearingly dysfunctional world of Chilean poets in this tender and insightful novel about love, art, and chosen family.

## MULTIPLE CHOICE

Written in the form of a standardized test, *Multiple Choice* invites the reader to respond to virtuoso language exercises and short narrative passages through questions that are thought-provoking, usually unanswerable, and often absurd. Poignant and political, *Multiple Choice* explores the nature of storytelling, authoritarianism and its legacies, and the way in which, rather than learning to think for ourselves, we are trained to obey and repeat.